Olivia by the Ocean

The Sound of Long O

by Cecilia Minden and Joanne Meier • illustrated by Bob Ostrom

The Child's World

Published by The Child's World®
1980 Lookout Drive
Mankato, MN 56003-1705
800-599-READ
www.childsworld.com

The Child's World®: Mary Berendes, Publishing Director
The Design Lab: Design and page production

Library of Congress Cataloging-in-Publication Data
  Minden, Cecilia.
    Olivia by the ocean : the sound of long O / by Cecilia
Minden and Joanne Meier ; illustrated by Bob Ostrom.
      p. cm.
    ISBN 978-1-60253-412-4 (library bound : alk. paper)
  1. English language—Vowels—Juvenile literature.
  2. English language—Phonetics—Juvenile literature
  3. Reading—Phonetic method—Juvenile literature.
  I. Meier, Joanne D. II. Ostrom, Bob, ill. III. Title.
    PE1157.M547 2010
    [E]—dc22   2010013396

Printed in the United States of America in Mankato, MN.
July 2010
F11538

NOTE TO PARENTS AND EDUCATORS:

The Child's World® has created this series with the goal of exposing children to engaging stories and illustrations that assist in phonics development. The books in the series will help children learn the relationships between the letters of written language and the individual sounds of spoken language. This contact helps children learn to use these relationships to read and write words.

The books in this series follow a similar format. An introductory page, to be read by an adult, introduces the child to the phonics feature, or sound, that will be highlighted in the book. Read this page to the child, stressing the phonic feature. Help the student learn how to form the sound with her mouth. The story and engaging illustrations follow the introduction. At the end of the story, word lists categorize the feature words into their phonic elements.

Each book in this series has been carefully written to meet specific readability requirements. Close attention has been paid to elements such as word count, sentence length, and vocabulary. Readability formulas measure the ease with which the text can be read and understood. Each book in this series has been analyzed using the Spache readability formula.

Reading research suggests that systematic phonics instruction can greatly improve students' word recognition, spelling, and comprehension skills. This series assists in the teaching of phonics by providing students with important opportunities to apply their knowledge of phonics as they read words, sentences, and text.

The letter o makes two sounds.

The short sound of o sounds like o as in: *job* and *box*.

The long sound of o sounds like o as in: *open* and *rope*.

In this book, you will read words that have the long o sound as in: *ocean, stone, toes,* and *home*.

Olivia lives by the ocean. She is going to walk by the water.

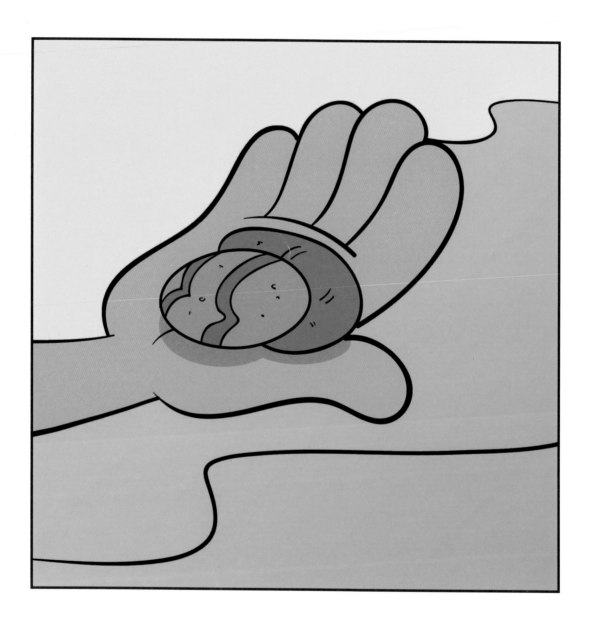

She finds some stones.

Those stones are so pretty!

She pokes her toes in
the water.
Oh, the water feels good!

Olivia walks over to a
little puppy.
"Are you all alone,
little puppy?"
She pets the puppy's
soft nose.

Here comes Olivia's friend, Toby.

"You found my puppy, Pokey," says Toby.

"I left the door open.
Pokey ran out. Thank you
for finding him," says Toby.

"I also have a puppy. Her name is Opal," says Olivia.

It is time for Olivia to

go home.

Olivia waves to Toby
and Pokey.

"I hope I see you tomorrow!"

Fun Facts

The Pacific Ocean is the world's largest ocean, and it is also the deepest. This ocean touches four continents—North America, South America, Asia, and Australia. Other major oceans are the Atlantic, the Indian, and the Arctic. Unlike the water in most lakes and rivers, the water in oceans contains salt. Some plants and animals are able to live only in freshwater, while others are able to live only in saltwater.

If your parents own a toolbox, you might notice that most of the tools are made of metal. But people didn't always work with metal tools. Two to five million years ago, they used tools made of bone, wood, and stone. For this reason, that period of time became known as the Stone Age.

Activity

Learning about Your Birthstone
Every month has a precious stone, or gem, that is known as a *birthstone*. If you were born in January, your birthstone is a red stone known as a garnet. The birthstone for April is a diamond. If you were born in September, your birthstone is a blue stone known as a sapphire. Find out what your birthstone is!

To Learn More

Books
About the Sound of Long O
Moncure, Jane Belk. *My "o" Sound Box®*. Mankato, MN: The Child's World, 2009.

About Oceans
Cole, Joanna, and Bruce Degen (illustrator). *The Magic School Bus on the Ocean Floor*. New York: Scholastic, 1992.

Ganeri, Anita. *I Wonder Why the Sea is Salty: and Other Questions About the Oceans*. New York: Kingfisher, 2003.

Gray, Samantha. *Eye Wonder: Ocean*. New York: DK Publishing, 2001.

About Stones
Lewis, Paul Owen. *The Jupiter Stone*. Berkeley, CA: Tricycle Press, 2003.

Plomer, Anna Llimós. *Stones and "Stuff."* Milwaukee, WI: Gareth Stevens, 2004.

Trimble, Marcia, and Susan Arciero (illustrator). *The Smiling Stone*. Los Altos Hills, CA: Images Press, 1998.

Web Sites
Visit our home page for lots of links about the Sound of Long O:

childsworld.com/links

Note to Parents, Teachers, and Librarians: We routinely check our Web links to make sure they're safe, active sites—so encourage your readers to check them out!

Long O Feature Words

Proper Names
Olivia	Pokey
Opal	Toby

Feature Words in Initial Position
ocean	open
oh	over

Feature Words with Consonant-Vowel-Silent E Pattern
alone	nose
home	poke
hope	stone

Feature Words with Other Vowel Patterns
go	so
going	toe

About the Authors

Cecilia Minden, PhD, is the former director of the Language and Literacy Program at the Harvard Graduate School of Education. She is now a reading consultant for school and library publications. She earned her PhD in reading education from the University of Virginia. Cecilia and her husband, Dave Cupp, live outside Chapel Hill, North Carolina. They enjoy sharing their love of reading with their grandchildren, Chelsea and Qadir.

Joanne Meier, PhD, has worked as an elementary school teacher, university professor, and researcher. She earned her BA in early childhood education from the University of South Carolina, and her MEd and PhD in education from the University of Virginia. She currently works as a literacy consultant for schools and private organizations. Joanne lives in Virginia with her husband Eric, daughters Kella and Erin, two cats, and a gerbil.

About the Illustrator

Bob Ostrom has been illustrating children's books for nearly twenty years. A graduate of the New England School of Art & Design at Suffolk University, Bob has worked for such companies as Disney, Nickelodeon, and Cartoon Network. He lives in North Carolina with his wife Melissa and three children, Will, Charlie, and Mae.